DORA'S STORYTIME COLLECTION

SIMON SPOTLIGHT
An imprint of Simon & Schuster Children's Publishing Division
1230 Avenue of the Americas, New York, New York 10020

DORA'S STORYTIME COLLECTION

Simon Spotlight/Nick Jr.

New York London Toronto Sydney

Contents

Little Star

adapted by Sarah Willson
illustrated by the Thompson Bros.

based on the teleplay by
Eric Weiner

¡Hola! I'm Dora and this is my friend Boots. Do you like to make wishes? Every night before I go to bed I make a wish on the first star I see in the sky. There's Little Star! Do you see her up there next to her friend the Moon?

Oh, no! A comet has just knocked Little Star out of the sky and she's falling to the ground.

We have to get Little Star back home to the Moon, so that everyone can make their wishes. Will you help us?

How can we get Little Star up to the moon? Let's ask the map. Say "Map!"

Map says we have to cross the Troll Bridge, then go past Tico's Tree, and that's how we'll get to Tall Mountain. If we climb Tall Mountain, we can take Little Star home to the Moon.

We made it to the Troll Bridge, but the Grumpy Old Troll won't let us go over his bridge unless we solve his riddle. Will you help us solve it?

The Grumpy Old Troll says, "Star light, star bright. Can you see the stars so bright? Star light, star bright, how many stars are there tonight?"

Can you count the stars? Don't forget to count Little Star!

Eleven stars! You solved the riddle! Thanks for helping. Now we can cross the bridge. Next is Tico's Tree. Do you see it?

¡Vámonos! Let's get Little Star home to the Moon, so everyone can make their wishes!

This is our friend Tico the squirrel's house. *¡Hola,* Tico! Uh-oh. I hear Swiper the fox! I think that sneaky fox is trying to swipe Little Star. If you see Swiper, say "Swiper, no swiping!"

You did it! You saved Little Star. Now we have to go to Tall Mountain. Do you see Tall Mountain?

There it is right underneath the Moon. Come on, we have to hurry! It's getting late!

We made it to the top of Tall Mountain! Little Star is almost home. But how are we going to get Little Star back up to the Moon? Let's stop and think.

I know! We can throw her back up to the moon! Can you help us?

Okay, cup your hands together. Now, on the count of three, I need you to throw your hands up in the air.

One . . . two . . . three. There she goes!

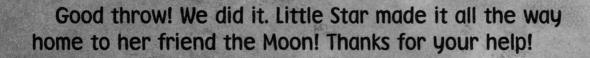

Good throw! We did it. Little Star made it all the way
home to her friend the Moon! Thanks for your help!

Now we can make our wishes.

Star light, star bright,
first star I see tonight.
I wish I may, I wish I might,
have this wish I wish tonight.

I wish that I could see Little Star every night.

Now you make your wish.

I hope it comes true! Good night!

NICK JR.

DORA the EXPLORER®

Dora's Backpack

adapted by Sarah Willson
illustrated by Robert Roper

based on the teleplay by
Eric Weiner

¡Hola! I'm Dora, and this is my friend Backpack! I need to return eight books to the library, and Backpack's going to help me. We have to get there before it closes. Will you help us too?

Great! First we need to find Boots the monkey. Do you see him?

Now we have to find the quickest way to the library. Who do we ask for help when we don't know which way to go? The Map! There's a map inside my Backpack. Say "Map!"

The Map says we have to go over the Troll Bridge and then cross Turtle River. That's how we'll get to the Library.

We made it to the Troll Bridge, but the Grumpy Old Troll won't let us cross unless we solve his riddle. Can you help us solve it?

"Here is one of my hardest quizzers," says the Grumpy Old Troll. "To cut through the net, use a pair of . . ." What do you think the answer is?

Scissors! That's right. Can you find a pair of scissors in my Backpack? We need them to cut through the net.

We did it! We made it over the Troll Bridge. So next comes Turtle River, but there's a storm cloud! It's going to rain!

Can you see if Backpack has something to keep us dry?

You found the umbrella!
Oh, no! That storm cloud made the ground
all wet. Now Boots is stuck in the Icky-Sticky Sand.

Let's check Backpack for something to help Boots. Can you find it?

Right, a rope! I need your help to pull Boots out. Use your hands and pull, pull, pull! Great job!

Now we need to take that boat across Turtle River. Before we get into the boat what should we wear to be safe? Check Backpack!

Right! Life jackets! Uh-oh. I hear Swiper the fox. He's trying to swipe them! If you see him, say "Swiper, no swiping!"

Thanks for helping us stop Swiper. Now we can cross Turtle River. We're almost at the library. Can you see it?

Here we are at the library.

Oh, no! The door is closed, but we can use Spanish to open it. If you say *"abre,"* the door will open. Can you say *"abre"*?

We did it! Now we can return my library books on time.

Can you count to make sure Val, the librarian, has all eight books from Backpack?

Hooray for Backpack! We couldn't have done it without
her or you! Thanks for helping!

Meet Diego!

by Leslie Valdes
illustrated by Susan Hall

based on the teleplay by
Eric Weiner

¡Hola! I'm Dora, and this is my friend, Boots. We're at the Animal Rescue Center, where they help all kinds of animals.

Eeep, eeep!

Errr, errr!

I hear a sound. Look—Baby Bear is about to fall out of the tree! Hang on, Baby Bear! Oh, no—he's falling!

Meow, meow!

Here comes my cousin, Diego. He's saving Baby Bear. Wow! Diego's really cool. He can make animal noises and talk to wild animals.

Can you say "Errrr, errrr!" to Baby Bear?

Uh-oh! Someone's calling for help. Diego's field journal helps him identify animals. Let's check it to figure out who's calling for help.

It's Baby Jaguar, and he's in trouble! We've got to get to the waterfall to help him!

Map says that to get to Baby Jaguar we need to go through the rain forest and past the cave, and that's how we'll get to the waterfall. Will you help us save Baby Jaguar? We have to hurry! *¡Vámonos!*

We made it to the rain forest! Look—there's a zip cord!
We can ride the zip cord through the treetops and zip through
the rain forest.

Do *you* see a ladder we can climb up?
Oh, no! The ladder is missing six rungs. Let's find the rungs.

Thanks for helping fix the ladder. Now let's go save Baby Jaguar. Wheee!

Meow, meow!

73

We made it to the cave! Do you see a polar bear?
Diego's journal says polar bears live only in the cold. But it's really, really hot in the rain forest. . . .

Oh, no! That's not a polar bear! Do you know who it is? It's Swiper, that sneaky fox. He'll try to swipe Diego's journal. We have to say "Swiper, no swiping!" Say it with me: "Swiper, no swiping!"

Thanks for helping us stop Swiper! Now we need to find the waterfall. We can use Diego's spotting scope to see things that are far away!

There's the waterfall. . . . And there's Baby Jagua
We're coming, Baby Jaguar!

We can water-ski down the river to save Baby Jaguar.
Diego says if we ask the dolphin, he'll pull us through the water.
Can you help me call the dolphin? Say "Click, click!" Again!

Click, click!

The dolphin can pull us through the river, but we need
something to hold on to. Let's check Backpack! Say "Backpack!"
What can the dolphin use to pull us along the water?

A rope! *¡Excelente!* We all need to hold on to the rope. Put your hands out in front of you and hold on tight. Whoaaaa!

Yeah! We made it to the other side of the river.
Oh, no! Baby Jaguar is about to fall over the giant waterfall!
Diego says the big condors can help us: They can fly us all the way
to Baby Jaguar. Say "Squawk, squawk!" to call the big condors!

Squawk, squawk!

Quick! You have to help us fly to Baby Jaguar!
Flap your arms. Faster!

Meow!

83

Hooray! We caught him!

We saved Baby Jaguar, and now the whole Jaguar family is together again. Thanks for helping!

Happy Birthday, Mami!

adapted by Leslie Valdes
illustrated by Jason Fruchter

based on the teleplay by
Leslie Valdes

¡Hola! Today is my *mami's* birthday. I'm making a special cake for my *mami* to show her how much I love her. Will you help me make it? Great!

First we need to find the recipe card for the banana-nut-chocolate cake. Do you see the recipe card that has bananas, nuts, and chocolate?

Here's the recipe card! But where can we find bananas, nuts, and chocolate? Let's ask the Map. Say "Map!"

Map says we have to go to the Banana Grove, then through the Nutty Forest, and finally to the Chocolate Tree! Then we'll have all the ingredients to make my *mami's* cake.

It's my friend Boots the monkey and his mommy! Boots drew a picture of himself with his mommy. Nice drawing, Boots!

Come on, let's go to the Banana Grove! Do you see the grove?

We made it to the Banana Grove. We need three bananas for the cake. The bananas need to be yellow—that means they're ripe! Do you see three yellow bananas?

Good counting!

Hey, look, it's our friend Benny the bull with his Grandma. Hi, Benny! Benny's giving his grandma a big hug because he loves her so much.

¡Vámonos! Let's go to the Nutty Forest. We still have to get the other ingredients. Bye, Benny!

Here we are at the Nutty Forest. And there's our friend Tico the squirrel and his mommy. They're gathering nuts together. They love nuts!

We need to collect six nuts for our cake. Let's count them in Spanish: ¡uno, dos, tres, cuatro, cinco, seis!

You did it! Good counting!

Here's our friend Isa the iguana. Hi, Isa! Isa is picking flowers for her mommy. Isa's mommy loves flowers just like Isa does!

Oh, no! Look! There's Swiper the fox. That sneaky fox is trying to swipe Isa's flowers. Say "Swiper, no swiping!"

You did it! You saved Isa's flowers!
Now we have to go to the Chocolate
Tree. Do you see it?

Come on, let's go get the last ingredient for my *mami's* special cake!

We made it to the Chocolate Tree! It only has one piece of chocolate left, and it's way up high. Can you help us reach it? Put your hands in the air and reach really high!

Yay! You reached the chocolate! Now we have all the ingredients. Let's go home and make the cake.

This is my daddy, *mi papi*. He's going to help us make the cake. First we put all the ingredients into a bowl and mix them up. *¡Bate, bate, bate!* Mix, mix, mix!

After we mix all the ingredients *Papi* will put the cake in the oven to bake. The cake will be ready soon. Thanks for helping!

It's time to give my *mami* the special cake!

Mami says it's delicious—
¡delicioso!

Happy Birthday, *Mami!* I love you!

Dora Saves the Prince

adapted by Alison Inches   based on a teleplay by Valerie Walsh
illustrated by Brian McGee

¡Hola! I'm Dora and this is my friend Boots. A mean witch cast a spell and put Prince Ramón in the Stone Tower. We're going to save him.

Map says we have to go through the Dark Forest, over Tall Mountain, and that's how we'll get to the Stone Tower. Will you help us? Thanks!

There's the Dark Forest! What do we need to find our way in the dark?

A light! Check Backpack for something we can use to light up the Dark Forest.

We made it through the Dark Forest! Now we need to get over Tall Mountain, but the witch cast a spell and stopped the train. If we say "go" in Spanish, it will move. Will you say *"sigue"*? Say it again!

We made it over Tall Mountain! Now we need to bring Prince Ramón down from the Stone Tower.

1

There should be eight steps, but the witch cast a spell and took away three of the steps.

8

6

4

3

If you can figure out which number steps are missing, we'll be able to walk up!

You figured out the missing numbers! *¡Lo hicimos!* We did it! We climbed up the steps and rescued Prince Ramón!

Hooray!

Thanks for helping!

Dora's Treasure Hunt

NICK JR.
DORA the EXPLORER

adapted by Alison Inches   based on a teleplay by Eric Weiner
illustrated by Susan Hall

¡Hola! I'm Dora and this is my friend Boots. We're going on a treasure hunt! Will you help us find the way to Treasure Island? Great!

Map says we have to go over the Icky-Sticky Sand, cross Crocodile Lake, and that's how we get to Treasure Island!

Treasure Island

Crocodile Lake

Icky-Sticky Sand

First we have to cross
the Icky-Sticky Sand, but
the bridge is broken.
Will you find the missing
pieces?

Thanks for helping us get over the Icky-Sticky Sand.

We can use that boat to get across Crocodile Lake. What should we wear so we can be safe?

We made it to Treasure Island! What do we need to open the treasure chest?

A key! Check Backpack for a key with three points, so we can open the treasure chest.

¡Lo hicimos! We did it!

We opened the treasure chest!
Look at all the treasure inside. Hooray!

NICK JR.

DORA the EXPLORER

Good Night, Dora!

by Christine Ricci
illustrated by Susan Hall

¡Hola! I'm Dora. Boots is coming to my house for a sleepover tonight. Look! The Bugga Bugga Babies are almost asleep. Can you whisper "good night"? Now whisper it in Spanish: *"buenas noches."*

"Peep! Peep! Peep!" The birds are peeping good night! Say good night to the birds!

Peep

Peep Peep

¡Buenas noches, pájaros!

Let's go home. First we have to go through the Flowery Garden. I hear a noise coming from those flowers. "Buzz! Buzz! Buzz!" The bees are buzzing good night! Will you say good night to the bees?

Oh, I hear something coming from the barn. "Cluck! Cluck! Cluck!" The chickens are clucking good night! Let's say good night to the chickens. *¡Buenas noches, pollos!*

Wait! Someone's next to the log. "Squeak! Squeak! Squeak!" The mice are squeaking good night! Say good night to the mice!

Squeak

Squeak

Squeak

¡Buenas noches, ratones!

Wheeeeee! Oh! I think I hear something.
"Hiss! Hiss! Hiss!" The snakes are hissing good
night! Will you say good night to the snakes?

¡Buenas noches, culebras!

Hiss

Hiss

Hiss

149

Hey, someone's making a sound in the pond. "Ribbet! Ribbet!" The frogs are croaking good night! Let's say good night to them.

Ribbet

Ribbet

¡Buenas noches, ranas!

Hoot

Hoot

Hoot

We're almost home. We just have to get over this bridge. Oh, I hear something. . . . "Hoot! Hoot! Hoot!" The owl is hooting good night. Let's say good night to the owl! *¡Buenas noches, lechuza!*

Yay! We're home. Good night,
Boots! *¡Buenas noches, Mami!* And
good night to you, too! *¡Buenas
noches!*

Say it in Spanish!

abre	open	AH-bray
abejas	bees	ah-BAY-hahs
bate	mix	BAH-tay
buenas noches	good night	BWEH-nahs NOH-cheys
cinco	five	SIN-koh
cuatro	four	KWAH-troh
culebras	snakes	coo-LAY-brahs
delicioso	delicious	deh-lee-see-OH-soh
dos	two	DOHS
excelente	excellent	ex-seh-LEN-tay
hola	hello	OH-lah
lechuza	owl	lay-CHOO-sah

Dilo en Español!!

lo hicimos	we did it	LOH ee-SEE-mohs
mami	mother	MAH-mee
papi	father	PAH-pee
pájaros	birds	PAH-hah-rohs
pollos	chickens	POH-yohs
ratones	mice	rah-TOHN-ays
ranas	frogs	RAH-nahs
seis	six	SEYS
sigue	go	SEE-gay
tres	three	TREHS
uno	one	OO-noh
vámonos	let's go	VAH-moh-nohs